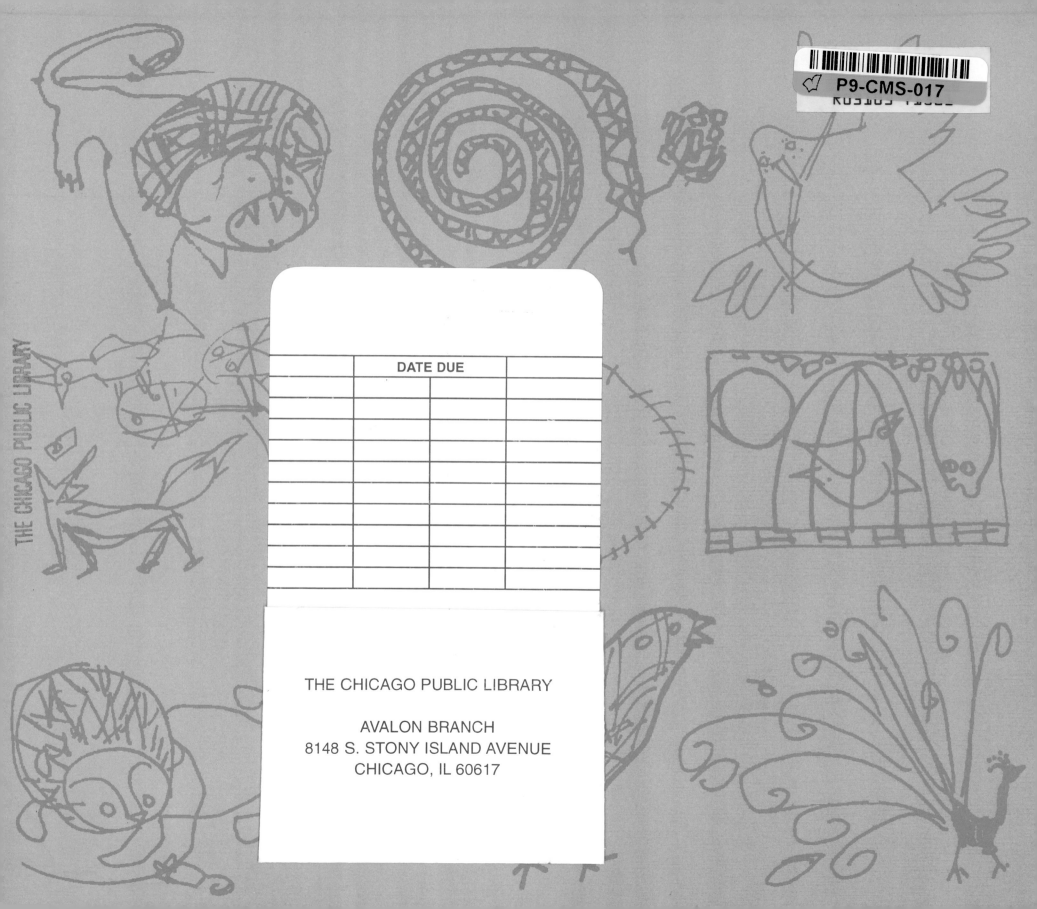

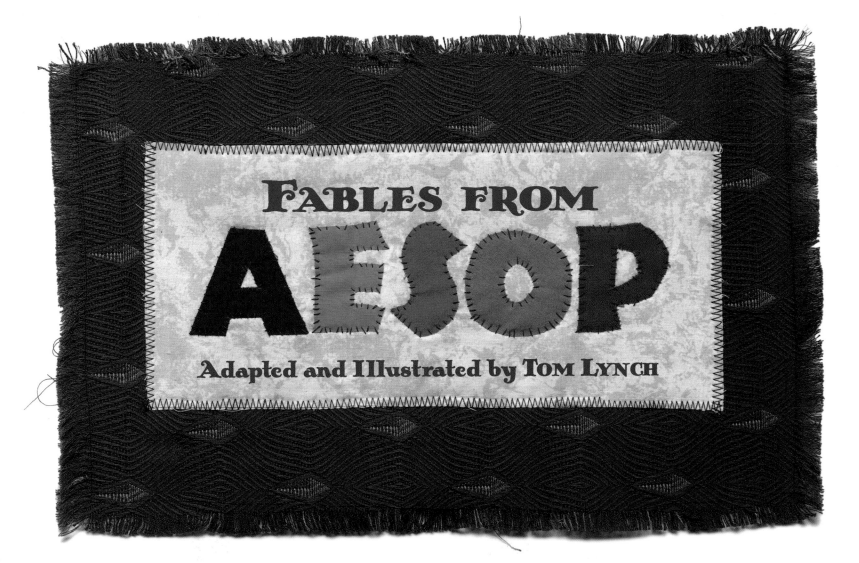

FABLES FROM AESOP

Adapted and Illustrated by TOM LYNCH

VIKING

This book could not have been completed without the

knowledge and inspiration of David J. Passalacqua, my teacher and friend

and the

assistance and encouragement of Antonio Reonegro, my best friend.

My sincerest thanks and appreciation.

T.L.

VIKING
Published by the Penguin Group
Penguin Putnam Books for Young Readers, 345 Hudson Street, New York, New York 10014, U.S.A.
Penguin Books Ltd, 27 Wrights Lane, London W8 5TZ, England
Penguin Books Australia Ltd, Ringwood, Victoria, Australia
Penguin Books Canada Ltd, 10 Alcorn Avenue, Toronto, Ontario, Canada M4V 3B2
Penguin Books (N.Z.) Ltd, 182-190 Wairau Road, Auckland 10, New Zealand

Penguin Books Ltd, Registered Offices: Harmondsworth, Middlesex, England

First published in 2000 by Viking, a division of Penguin Putnam Books for Young Readers.

3 5 7 9 10 8 6 4 2

Illustrations copyright © Tom Lynch, 2000
All rights reserved
The author found the translations of V. S. Vernon Jones in *Aesop's Fables*,
Penguin, 1995, particularly helpful in preparing these adaptations.

LIBRARY OF CONGRESS CATALOGING-IN-PUBLICATION DATA
Aesop's fables. English. Selections.
Fables from Aesop / illustrated by Tom Lynch.
p.   cm.
Summary: A collection of familiar short moral tales.
ISBN 0-670-88948-2 (hardcover)
1. Fables, Greek—Translations into English. [1. Fables. 2.
Folklore.] I. Aesop. II. Lynch, Tom (Tom A.), ill. III. Title.
PZ8.2 .F337 2000
398.24'52—dc21   00-008088

Printed in Hong Kong
Set in Schneidler

About the artwork:
The artwork for this book was hand sewn using new and used fabrics of all kinds.
The thumbnail sketches for some of the pieces are printed on the end pages.

To my wife Christine,
for Thomas.

With Noses and 'Sammich Kisses.

THE TORTOISE AND THE HARE

One day a Hare was teasing a Tortoise for being so slow on his feet.

"Hold on there," said the Tortoise. "I'll bet if we had a race I would win!"

"You've got to be kidding!" laughed the Hare. "Okay slowpoke, let's go!"

They both started off at the same time, but very soon the Hare was so far ahead of the Tortoise that he thought he might as well rest for a bit. Before he knew it, he had fallen fast asleep. All the while, the Tortoise continued to move slowly along. Mile after mile he crept, and in time he reached the finish line. Eventually the Hare awoke and jumped up to continue as fast as he could. But he reached the finish line only to find that the Tortoise had arrived before him and won the race.

So remember! Slow and steady wins the race.

A LESSON FOR A FOOLISH CROW

One day a Crow stole a piece of cheese from a hunter's lunch and perched herself in a tree to eat it. A passing Fox saw the cheese in the Crow's beak and was determined to get it for himself. So he crept under the tree and sweetly called up to her: "Oh my, Miss Crow! How beautiful you are! Your dark, shiny feathers! Your lovely, delicate feet! Why, if a queen ruled all the creatures in the woods, it should be you! Surely your voice must match your beauty! Oh, what I would not give to hear a beautiful song from your throat!"

The Crow was thrilled. She was so eager to show off her voice that she opened her beak, let go of the cheese, and croaked as loudly as she could.

"CAW! CAW! CAAAWW!!!"

"Ah ha!" thought the Fox as he jumped and snapped up the cheese.

And as he walked off, the sneaky Fox laughed. "If you only had brains as well as beauty, Miss Crow, you would make an excellent queen!"

So remember! Don't always believe what you hear.

MONKEY SEE, MONKEY DO

The Monkey sat up in his tree near the water and watched the fishermen cast their nets empty and pull them back full of fish. "Why, I'm sure I could do that, too!" he thought. "It looks so easy!"

So when the fishermen went off for their lunch, the Monkey came down from his tree, grabbed the net, and tried to copy them. But he soon became tangled up in the net, fell into the water, and almost drowned.

"Oh dear!" he said. "That's what I deserve for trying to fish when I really had no idea how to do it!"

**So remember!
Nothing is gained without
knowledge and practice.**

THE SUFFERING FOX

One day a Fox who was crossing the river got swept up by the current and carried off into a deep marsh. All his struggles to get out were useless. He was stuck, muddy, wet, and cold. And to add to his misery, he was attacked by a swarm of ticks which clung to him and bit him. A Hedgehog came by and felt sorry for him. Too little to help the Fox out of the marsh, she offered to pick the ticks out of his fur for him. "Oh, please don't do that!" begged the Fox.

"But why not?" asked the Hedgehog.

"Because these ticks have had a fine feast and are not hungry any longer. But if you pull them off, another hungry bunch will come and take their place!"

So remember! New troubles will replace your old ones if you do not overcome them.

A LESSON LEARNED TOO LATE

A Songbird hung in her cage outside a window. Every night she would sing when all the other birds were asleep. A Bat came every night and clung to the bars of the cage to listen. One night he asked her why she was silent all day and only sang her songs at night.

"I used to do all my singing in the daytime," said the Songbird. "But a hunter was attracted by my voice and set out a net to catch me. Since then, I've learned my lesson! Now I sing only at night."

But the Bat chuckled and said, "You've learned your lesson *too late*, my dear! It's no use being careful now, when you are a prisoner. If you had been careful *before* you were caught, you might still be free."

So remember! Regrets and precautions are useless after misfortune has come.

THE UNWELCOME GUEST

Long ago, the mighty god Zeus was celebrating his wedding day. Every animal in the world brought a gift to him. Even the Snake held a rose in his sharp fangs and crawled up to Mount Olympus. But Zeus took one look at him and said, "I welcome gifts from all the world's creatures, but from *you* Mr. Snake, I want nothing!"

So remember! Never accept the offerings of a villain.

A TIME FOR PATIENCE

Sniffing for food one day, a hungry Fox came upon a shepherd's lunch sack hidden in a hollow old tree. So he squeezed into the tree and gobbled up all the bread and meat that he found. But his belly became so full that the Fox could not fit through the hole in the tree again. As much as he tried, he could not get out.

Hearing him cry out, another Fox came running to help.

"Why don't you stay in there for a while?" said the other Fox. "Wait until you get as thin as you were when you first went in; then you'll be able to slip out easily!"

So remember!
Time and patience can solve
many problems.

THE GENTLE ART OF PERSUASION

The Sun and the North Wind were always arguing over who was more powerful. One day they decided to settle the dispute once and for all. They agreed that the one who could strip a traveler of his clothing would be declared most powerful. The North Wind was the first to try. He blew and blew, but the gusts of wind only made the unsuspecting traveler pull his clothes around him more tightly. When the Wind blew harder still, the cold made the man put on another coat. Finally the Wind grew tired. It was the Sun's turn to try.

First the Sun shone with a gentle warmth; the man took off his extra coat. Then the Sun blazed brighter and brighter until, unable to stand the heat, the traveler stripped off all his clothes and went to a nearby river for a cool swim.

So remember! Often gentle persuasion works better than brute force.

THE RISKY VISIT

A feeble old Lion found an easy way to hunt for food.

He stayed in his cave and pretended to be very sick. When any visitor came into the cave to ask about his health, he leaped on them and ate them up.

One day the Fox came to the outside of the cave. He stuck only his head in and asked the Lion how he was doing.

"Oh, I'm not feeling well at all, my little friend," the Lion said. "But come on in! Why do you stand outside?"

"I would come inside," said the Fox, "but I see all these footprints on the ground. And they are all going *into* your cave but none of them are coming *out*!"

So remember!
Learn to recognize trouble
before it leads to danger.

THE FOX AND THE THIRSTY GOAT

One day a Fox fell into a water tank and was unable to get himself out. Soon a thirsty Goat came by, and saw the Fox in the tank.

"Fox," he called. "Is the water good?"

"Good?" said the Fox. "Why, this is the best water I've ever tasted in my whole life! Why don't you come down and get some for yourself?"

The Goat jumped right down. But after he had had enough to drink, he, too, could find no way out of the tank. "I have an idea!" said the Fox. "Let me climb up onto your horns; then I can climb out. Once I'm free I'll help you."

The Goat agreed, but when the Fox climbed up and out to freedom, he chuckled and just walked away. The Goat called out loudly, "Hey! Hey Fox! What about me?"

But the Fox laughed and said, "If you had as much sense in your head as you have hair in your beard you wouldn't have jumped down in there before you figured out how to get back up again!"

So remember! Look before you leap.

THE LION AND THE MOUSE

A sleeping Lion was awakened one morning by a Mouse running over his face. The Lion became so angry that he grabbed the little Mouse in his paws and was about to eat him up. The terrified Mouse begged for his life.

"Please let me go!" he cried. "If you do, one day I will repay you for your kindness!" The idea of such an insignificant little creature ever being able to do anything for him amused the Lion so much that he laughed out loud and good-humoredly let the Mouse go.

Then one day the Lion got caught in a snare set by a hunter and was unable to get himself free. The Mouse heard and recognized the Lion's angry roars and ran to the spot where he was. He went right to work gnawing at the ropes with his teeth. Soon the Lion was set free.

"You see! You laughed at me when I promised I would repay you. But now you see that even a little Mouse can help a Lion!"

So remember!
No act of kindness, however small, is ever wasted.

THE PEACOCK AND THE SPARROW

One day a Peacock was teasing a Sparrow about the dullness of her plumage. "Look at my brilliant colors," he said, "and see how much finer they are than your poor feathers. I am dressed in gold and purple, and my patterns are dazzling! But your wings are drab and plain!"

"You're right," replied the Sparrow. "Your feathers are far more beautiful than mine, but when it comes to flying, my wings let me soar into the clouds and up to the heavens. You are stuck to the earth like any other barnyard fowl."

And the Peacock sadly watched as the Sparrow flew off.

So remember! Ability is more important than a splendid display.

THE FOX AND HIS SHADOW

A Fox found himself on an open plain one day as the sun was setting. He was surprised to see his own long shadow. "Well! I never knew what a big fellow I really am!" he said. "Imagine *me* being afraid of a lion! Why, I am many feet tall! I'm such a giant, I am sure that I could make myself the king of all the creatures in the woods!"

Just then a hungry Lion came sneaking up behind him and caught the Fox in his paws, ready to eat him up.

Too late, the Fox was sorry for his mistake. "Oh no! All my silly bragging has gotten little me into a big mess!"

**So remember!
A false appearance,
no matter how believable,
is no match for the real thing.**

ABOUT AESOP

Born in Greece, Aesop lived as a slave in the sixth century B.C. He possessed great wit and gained a reputation for telling clever animal tales that amused and impressed those who heard them. He was freed by his masters on account of his intelligence. Because he never wrote any of his fables down, it is impossible to say which fables are actually his. Throughout the centuries, his name became the legendary one to which many fables are credited.

The fables of Aesop seek to teach virtues that will make life better for those who choose to practice them. Loyalty, gratitude, kindness, and modesty are some of the values common to Aesop's universal wisdom.